THE LAST WORD

By Michael Dahl

Illustrated by
Bradford Kendall

STONE ARCH BOOKS
a capstone imprint

The Library of Doom: The Final Chapters is published by
Stone Arch Books
A Capstone Imprint
1710 Roe Crest Drive
North Mankato, Minnesota 56003
www.mycapstone.com

Cataloging-in-Publication Data is available at the Library of Congress website.

ISBN: 978-1-4965-2559-8 (library binding)
ISBN: 978-1-4965-2571-0 (eBook)
Designer: Hilary Wacholz

Summary: In the heart of the Library of Doom, within the Librarian's secret
chamber, is a sealed, invisible vault. It contains a single book — a book so
poisonous that it drains the Librarian's life away day by day, year by year. It is
the price each Librarian must pay, because if anyone reads the final word in the
story, the whole world will be destroyed! So when the book goes missing, the
Librarian must track it down without delay. There's just one problem: only another
Librarian would know where the book was located. Is there a traitor in the League
of Librarians?

Printed in US.
007527CGS16

These are the last days of the Library of Doom.

The forces of villainy are freeing the Library's most dangerous books. Only one thing can stop Evil from penning history's final chapter — the League of Librarians, a mysterious collection of heroes who only appear when the Library faces its greatest threat.

Never underestimate the power of words.

TABLE OF CONTENTS

Chapter 1

THE ONLY WAY DOWN

The Diamond Page stands **TALL** next to a deep well. He peers over the edge.

The top branches of a gigantic tree poke out. It is the great Word Tree.

Its roots grow from the deepest chamber of the Library of Doom.

Seven days ago, the Librarian left. He climbed down the Word Tree.

He went to check on a book. It is hidden at the very bottom.

The book is **evil**. When the Librarian is close to it, he loses some of his life.

The Librarian told the Diamond Page to wait for him.

The Page has waited for seven days. He sighs. "I'm tired of waiting," he says.

He is **worried**. Something has happened to the Librarian.

Something **BAD**.

"There's only one way down," the Diamond Page says.

Chapter 2

THE ONLY
WAY BACK

The Diamond Page leaps. He **sails** over the edge of the well.

Thunk! His diamond boots land on a thick branch.

The bark is as hard as **ROCK**.

The page carefully climbs down the Tree.

A **breeze** whistles through the branches.

The Tree's leaves rustle. They whisper to the Diamond Page.

It is hard to make out the quiet words.

"Turn 'round," the leaves whisper. "The only way is back."

The Diamond Page shakes his head. "No," he said. "I will not turn back."

The leaves rustle once more. "Be wise, below," they whisper.

The Diamond Page frowns. But he keeps climbing down.

His muscles grow tired.

How long have I been climbing? he wonders.

He stops to rest on a **HUGE** branch.

He looks down. Light shines at the bottom.

A pool of water **shimmers** near the Tree's roots.

And near the pool is a dark figure. It is not moving.

It is the Librarian.

Chapter 3

UNDERWATER

The Diamond Page drops onto the grass next to the Librarian.

There is **blood** on the Librarian's face and hands.

"Oh, no," the Page says. "I'm too late."

The Page looks around. "But where is the book?" he says.

His diamond armor **SHINES** in the light. It reflects on the Librarian's face.

The Librarian suddenly takes a breath.

A low **groan** escapes his mouth.

The Librarian tries hard to speak. He points to the **water**.

"Pool," he says. "In . . . the pool."

Bubbles appear on the water's surface.

The Diamond Page stands. "Is that where the book is hidden?" he asks.

The Librarian nods.

The Page runs. He leaps.

Splash! He dives into the pool.

The Diamond Page dives down. **DEEPER** he goes. He spots another swimmer.

The swimmer is rising to meet him. His hand clutches a glowing red book.

It is the evil book. The Last Word.

The Diamond Page grabs the book. He pulls.

The other swimmer will not let go.

They wrestle in the water.

Bubbles swirl around them.

WHOOSH!

They both reach the pool's surface.

The Page **gasps** for air.

Now he can see the other man's face.

"The Collector!" the Page cries.

Chapter 4

THE LAST WORD

The Collector **HITS** the Diamond Page with the book.

The Page falls. He slams into the trunk of the Tree.

"The Last Word is mine," says the villain.
"Now listen to me read."

The Diamond Page slides to the ground.

His **STRENGTH** is suddenly gone.

"The book is **draining** both your lives," says the Collector.

He holds up the glowing book. He laughs.

"I will read the last word in this book," he says. "It will destroy the world!"

"Why?" asks the Page. "If the world is destroyed, you will be, too."

The Collector grins. "This is the last book I need for my collection," he says. "It is complete now. My task is finished. I have **WON**!"

The Collector's wicked laugh echoes across the pool.

He opens the red book. He turns to the last page.

All is silent.

The wind **blows** above the Page's head.

The leaves rustle. Ink drips from them.

The ink oozes into the page's hair.

His strength **RETURNS**.

He jumps up. He leaps across the pool.

The Collector tries to run.

The page grabs the book. He holds it, open, in front of him.

"You fool!" cries the Collector. He points at the Page's shining armor. "I can still read the last page!"

The Diamond Page does not close the book. He does not move.

The Collector **smiles**. Quickly, he reads aloud. "The last word is —"

The Diamond Page opens his eyes.

The Collector is **GONE**.

The red book rests on the grass by the pool.

The Librarian stands. He walks over to the Page. "My strength is back," he says. "What happened?"

The Diamond Page grins.

"He read the last word reflected in my armor," says the young hero. "But he read it backward. Like in a mirror."

"Turn around," the leaves whisper.

The Diamond Page nods. "The only way is back," he answers.

GLOSSARY

diamond (DAHY-muhnd)—a very hard, usually colorless stone that is a form of carbon and is often used in expensive jewelry

draining (DRAYN-ing)—emptying or stealing energy from something

page (PAYJ)—one side of a sheet of paper in an open book. Also, a page is a young boy or girl who works as a servant or assistant for an important person.

shimmer (SHIM-er-ing)—shining light that seems to move slightly

silent (SAHY-luhnt)—completely quiet or without noise

swirl (SWURL)—to move in circles or cause something to move in circles. Also, a circular pattern.

wise (WAHYZ)—having or showing wisdom or knowledge usually from learning or experiencing many things

DISCUSSION QUESTIONS

1. When the Librarian is lying by the pool, the Diamond Page sees blood on him. What do you think happened?

2. Do you think the Word Tree was alive? Are there places in the story that provide clues?

3. How does the Diamond Page know how to trick the Collector? Can you tell at which point in the story the Page gets his idea?

WRITING PROMPTS

1. The Librarian hid the evil book deep in the pool by the Word Tree. Can you think of another good hiding place? Tell us where else you would hide it.

2. The Diamond Page wears very special armor. It seems to have magical powers. Make a list of the powers you think the page has because of his armor.

3. The Word Tree is the tallest tree in the world. Write a paragraph about your own adventure climbing the tree. What do you discover? Are there other treasures or creatures living in the Tree?

THE AUTHOR

Michael Dahl is the prolific author of the bestselling *Goodnight, Baseball* picture book and more than 200 other books for children and young adults. He has won the AEP Distinguished Achievement Award three times for his nonfiction, a Teachers' Choice Award from *Learning* magazine, and a Seal of Excellence from the Creative Child Awards. He is also the author of the Hocus Pocus Hotel mystery series and the Dragonblood books. Dahl currently lives in Minneapolis, Minnesota.

THE ILLUSTRATOR

Bradford Kendall has enjoyed drawing for as long as he can remember. As a boy, he loved to read comic books and watch old monster movies. He graduated from the Rhode Island School of Design with a BFA in Illustration. He has owned his own commercial art business since 1983. Bradford lives in Providence, Rhode Island, with his wife, Leigh, and their two children, Lily and Stephen.